Pup on the Pitch

Other books in the same series:

Bobby, Charlton and the Mountain

'An excellent story . . . the first-person voice of the narrator is so immediate, so animated.'

TES

Man of the Match

Shortlisted for the Highland Children's Book Awards.

Selected by Chelsea Football Club as the nominated title in a reading scheme run in association with the National Literacy Trust.

Team Trouble

'Simple and unpretentious, this novel manages to convey the warmth and humour of family life.'

School Librarian

Pirates Ahoy!

Footballs double as cannonballs when this football-mad family get piratical at the beach!

Pup on the Pitch

SOPHIE SMILEY

Illustrated by
MICHAEL FOREMAN

Andersen Press
London

First published in Great Britain in 2009
by Andersen Press Limited,
20 Vauxhall Bridge Road, London SW1V 2SA
www.andersenpress.co.uk

British Library Cataloguing in Publication Data available.
ISBN 978 184 270 883 5

Printed and bound in Great Britain by
CPI Bookmarque Ltd., Croydon, Surrey

To Titch Minter, and the Berern Writing Group

and

Sean and Owen Connors

DAVY
DOG
DAVY
DAVY
DOG

Chapter 1

There are so many dogs in our house that Mum says we should open a pets' home!

We have dogs on mugs, hats and T-shirts. You see, everyone in our house is football mad, and our club mascot is Davy Dog.

My brother, Bobby, loves our mascot, and kept asking for his own pet. More than anything he wanted a real, live Davy Dog.

But Mum said the house was too small. It is pretty full with my hairy big brothers, Wembley, Striker and Semi.

Mum and Dad tried to persuade him that little animals were just as good as big ones, and for Christmas they bought him a small, speedy pet.

'Call him "Goal Fish",' Striker said as Bobby watched his new friend swim round and round the tank. Semi built a goal from lolly sticks, and Wembley popped a ping-pong ball into the aquarium. Bobby sat for hours watching Goal Fish nudging the ball around, whispering, 'Shoot – shoot now, Goal Fish.'

Bobby's pet was a good footballer, but he wasn't soft or cuddly. And quite soon, the call 'Puppy? Puppy, please?' started again.

Then I heard our neighbour, old Mr Maskell (whom Bobby calls Mr Mascot), talking to Mum over the garden fence.

'I'm thinking of getting a dog,' he said, 'to help me with the chores.'

Mum nodded. 'I'm told they can do all sorts of things – even load the washing machine.'

But I had a better idea. What if the dog lived with Mr M but came to us on loan? Mr Maskell could be the team manager, and Bobby could be coach. He could even come to our house for away games. A kind of dog share scheme. A puppy would help me and Bobby with our football training – my team had the biggest match of the season coming up, and I needed all the help I could get. But I never dreamt that my fantastic plan would turn into a terrible own goal . . .

The day of the debut arrived.

Mr M came back from the animal rescue centre with a real, live Davy Dog perched in the basket of his electric ride-on. Bobby tore down the road and picked up the pup.

'Slowly, now,' Mr Maskell said. 'Give him time to get to know you, to learn your smell.'

‘I’m NOT smelly,’ Bobby said indignantly.

‘No, you’re not – but everyone has their own special smell, like a fingerprint.’

Bobby sniffed his fingers doubtfully.

‘Dogs have special powers,’ said Wembley.

‘Like Superman,’ said Striker.

‘Spiderman,’ Semi added.

‘Fly? Climb walls?’ Bobby asked.

‘Well, no,’ said Striker, ‘but they can hear sounds we can’t hear, and they remember people’s smells.’

‘So Davy Dog will always remember you,’ said Mr Maskell.

'He knows you're his special friend and he'll come to you if he's in trouble.'

Bobby beamed. 'Special friend,' he said, patting the pup. Davy wagged his tail, and seemed to grin. We weren't to know how quickly that special friendship would be put to the test.

Chapter 2

Mr Maskell settled down to a cup of tea and a piece of Mum's chocolate cake. Davy Dog wriggled in Bobby's arms. Then, struggling free, he jumped at the plate and gobbled up the whole cake. Bobby's face fell. Davy wagged his tail and seemed to be asking for more.

'Naughty dog!' Mr Maskell said, shaking his finger.

Davy hung his head, and looked just like Bobby when he's been naughty.

Bobby felt sorry for him. 'Play in our room?' he asked.

Oh dear . . .

Moments later, barks came from upstairs. I ran up and heard cries of 'Naughty dog!'

A terrible sight met my eyes. All Bobby's precious posters of his goalie hero, Will Brooks, were lying torn and chewed on the floor. Davy Dog leapt round the room, with the head of my favourite cuddly toy in his mouth. The stuffing sprayed around the room like snow. Bobby's lip trembled. His voice wobbled as he said,

'Give, Davy, give,' and shook his finger sternly.

But Davy thought it was just a new game. He frolicked in the soft snow, then jumped up at Bobby's finger as if it was a stick to catch.

'Let's take him into the garden and teach him football,' I said, desperate to get every bit of practice I could before my big match.

Davy bounded outside. He charged round in circles, ignoring Bobby's efforts to get him to pass the ball. Then he crouched in a corner, before chasing his tail again.

'Shoot, Davy Dog, shoot,' Bobby jigged in goal. But Davy just did more crouching, and twirling. He looked like one of those museum doors that whizz round and round.

'Get ready,' I shouted, kicking the ball. Bobby flew across the goal mouth. Whoosh! A brilliant save. I expected a whoop of 'Whaddasave!' Instead, there was a huge silence. Then a terrible wail.

I smelt him even before I saw the smears of dog dirt.

'Oh Bobs – all over your lovely goalie top.'

He pulled it off, muttering, 'Smelly, stinky, pooey poo!'

But Mum scooped it into the washing machine saying, 'It'll be as good as new in no time.' Then she added, 'I'm afraid that's what puppies do – they're like babies, they—'

'Stinky, smelly, greedy, pooey puppy,' Bobby growled.

Even Davy Dog seemed to

realise my brother was upset. He trotted up to say sorry, holding a punctured football as a present.

This time Bobby ignored the sad look on his face, marched to the drawer and pulled out Mum's referee kit. He blew her whistle, waved her red card, and shouted, 'Send him off!'

But Davy was one of those players who argue with the ref. Having made up his mind that Bobby was his special friend, he had no intention of leaving the pitch. And to show his feelings, he jumped up, licked Bobby all over, then piddled a puddle on his lap. When Bobby shrieked, he nipped him on the nose! That was it. Bobby never wanted to see a dog ever again. They were all monsters!

Chapter 3

My brother Bobby is the bravest person I know. He's the best goalie, too, because he's not afraid of anything. But after Davy Dog's visit, Fear crept into our house like a spy.

The next day, Bobby looked from left to right as he went out. He fidgeted on the wall while waiting for the taxi. (He goes to a special school 'cos he's got Down's syndrome. Mum says my school's special too, but I don't get to go in a taxi.)

Gradually he relaxed and swung his legs, singing, 'Football's comin' home, it's comin' 'ome . . .'

Suddenly, from round the corner, a dog appeared. Bobby

stiffened. A poodle wearing a pink coat came trip-trapping down the road. Her little pink nose was stuck in the air as if she was the poshest pooch in the world. I laughed, but Bobby stopped singing, and quickly drew his legs up onto the wall.

The dog approached. Stopped. Sniffed.

'I'm NOT smelly,' Bobby said crossly, adding, 'Red card – send off – pooey puppy!'

A fluffy pink lady appeared. She sniffed, and said, 'Matilda's a very sweet little doggy woggy.'

The poodle yapped and snapped at Bobby's toes.

'Come along, my precious,' the woman called, and they tottered off together.

Bobby didn't make a sound, but he froze. The dog trotted back for a last bark. Bobby put his hands over his face, and buried it in his lap.

'He thinks that if he can't see

the dog, then it can't see him,' Mum explained, and went out to give him a hug.

What an odd idea – putting your hands over your face to grow invisible. It was such a strange thought that it sat inside my head like a little seed.

But then a new menace came into sight: a horrible figure that I'd know anywhere. It was Kevin Joggs. What was worse, he'd seen what had happened. And as Bobby drove past in his taxi, Kevin jumped forward with a nasty grin and made 'Woof woof' noises. Bobby looked terrified.

Chapter 4

'Count to ten, Charlie,' Mum said, seeing my hands clench.

You see, I've got the biggest temper in the family, even though I'm the youngest and the only girl. I remembered how I'd let Mum and Dad down by beating Kevin up the last time he'd bullied my brother. Kevin made a gesture at the window which told me he hadn't forgotten our fight either.

Well, after Kevin and the poodle, Bobby wouldn't wait outside for the taxi any more. He kept watch from the sofa.

But on the day we went to the dentist, he skipped along happily singing, 'Toothbrush comin' home, it's comin',' and I began to think he was getting brave again.

He came out of the Tooth Fairy clinic looking pleased with himself. Mr Gums had given him a sticker and told him he'd got a great set of gnashers. Bobby walked along throwing his toothbrush into the air and catching it, when the noise started. The nightmare noise!

Bobby clutched Dad's arm. As we rounded the bend, we saw the biggest, sharpest set of toothy fangs ever. They stuck out of a gate, huge and pointy. The brute fixed its eyes on us and barked. Bobby leapt into Dad's arms, and I hid behind him. Saliva strings dripped from the dog's tongue, and he panted at us hungrily.

'Don't worry,' Dad said as we drew closer. 'He's just a guard dog, a defender; he's protecting his goal.'

The growls grew louder. We tiptoed forward. The teeth gleamed.

But Dad had given me an idea: if the dog was a goalie – well, I'm a striker, and in front of me was an empty can; with one quick movement I kicked it high over the gate and into the garden. The dog yelped, then bounded after it, and we dashed past.

'He's a useless goalie – not as good as you.' I tried to cheer Bobby up as we walked home.

But that dog had altered something in Bobby. He clung silently to Dad, and it seemed as if part of him had disappeared.

Chapter 5

Bobby changed. When I sang, 'Football's coming home, it's coming . . .', he didn't join in. So I tried, 'Knock knock,' but he wouldn't say, 'Who's there?' I even bought him a new poster of his goalie hero, but he hardly looked at it. He wouldn't do anything.

Yet when Gran said, 'Ooh, look, it's raining cats and dogs,' he went and hid under the sofa. And when

Dad told Semi, 'You're in the dog house,' Bobby's eyes filled with alarm. Then Mum bought a packet of doughnuts, and Bobby wouldn't eat them because he thought they said 'dog nuts'!

But there was still one thing left that was sure to cheer Bobby up, and that was a football match.

We all set off for the stadium waving our scarves and twirling our rattles, and Bobby smiled a little smile. Hooray, I thought, he's getting better. He shouted and cheered when our striker scored a hat-trick, and jiggled on the spot every time Will Brooks took a save.

As the match ended, he even began to hum.

Nobody dared offer him a hot dog, but he happily tucked into an ice cream.Everything felt good again, until I saw something that made my stomach turn a somersault: Kevin Joggs was watching us. He scowled, and then he chucked a bottle. There were shouts and pushes. Helmets sailed among the crowd. Two police dogs charged towards us, knocking Bobby over and sending his ice cream to the ground. Panic lit Bobby's face. It was like one of those dreams when your legs won't move. He was frozen. Kevin's face twisted into a mean smile as he pushed his way towards Bobby. Some big men moved forward, blocking me. What if they trampled on Bobby? What if Kevin got him? I was trapped; there was nothing I could do to save him.

Then, like a lifeguard, Wembley plunged into the sea of people, shoved Kevin to the side and scooped Bobby onto his shoulders and we began the long journey home. But once Bobby got home, he refused to go out.

Chapter 6

The taxi came and went, but Bobby wouldn't go to school. He hid under the sofa, perched on top of the wardrobe, and even locked himself in the loo. Mum blew her whistle, Dad flashed a red card, Wembley offered sweets, but nothing worked. Bobby wouldn't budge.

Every day Mr Maskell rode past with Davy on his way to dog training lessons.

‘Look, Davy Dog’s off to school,’ Mum said. ‘He’s learning to be a good helper.’

‘And a defender,’ I added. ‘Perhaps he’ll be a goalie like you. Come and play football?’

But Bobby wouldn’t even go into the garden in case Davy was on the other side of the fence.

Mum and Dad kept going into huddles, worrying about school. But I worried about missing football practice. You see, Bobby and I always play together, and I really needed his help. The next match was the one that would decide whether my team won the league.

Match day drew nearer. We did

everything we could to get Bobby outside. We tried nice things – sticker charts, new football boots, spaghetti and custard. We tried nasty things like early nights, naughty steps and no television.

But nothing would draw Bobby out of his shell.

Bobby had cheered me on in every match, and if he wasn't there, I was sure we'd play badly. I couldn't do it without him. We were doomed to lose.

Chapter 7

My big day arrived, and Bobby sat staring at Goal Fish.

'I can't play without you,' I said, crossly kicking a cushion. But Bobby didn't even look round, he didn't try to calm me down or tell me to 'count to ten'.

I was defeated. 'Ring up and say I'm sick,' I said.

'You can't let your team down.' Dad squeezed my hand.

Even Dad didn't understand. There was my football team, but Bobby and I are a team too. I put my head in my hands ready to howl.

But as my hands touched my face, I remembered something. When Bobby covered his face he thought no one could see him. It was my last hope.

'Bobs,' I cried, 'if you wear something over your face the dogs won't see you!'

An eye peeped out.

'You can come to the match – you'll be invisible – have special powers!'

A second eye stared at me. Then, very slowly, with his jumper pulled over his head, Bobby went upstairs. When he returned, he was wearing superhero pyjamas and a Halloween mask. 'Can't see me now,' he said bravely. 'I'm i'sivible.'

'In-sivible,' I agreed happily.

And for the first time in days, Bobby stepped out of the front door. Glancing nervously over his shoulder, and clinging to my arm, he crept along. He was still scared of his own shadow, but he was there beside me.

A crow cawed loudly, and Bobby jumped. He was a bag of nerves, and so was I. The opposition towered over us. Their striker was gigantic. She stared down at me and said, 'Hi, Titch.'

I was jittery for Bobby and jerky on the field. I just couldn't focus on the ball. But finally, I broke free, tore down the pitch and shouted, 'Pass, Fizza!' She placed the ball perfectly – right at my feet, and only the keeper stood between me and goal. A siren sounded and Bobby yelped. I shot wide. The ball thudded against the post and bounced away. Our first good chance and I'd blown it. I felt terrible.

Usually, when we watch each other, we send sort of magic beams onto the pitch which help us play better. But today Bobby was sending me great tidal waves of fear. I fumbled and fell over my feet. I went offside. Crashed into the goalpost. Every minute I was expecting to be subbed off. And as the match stretched out, Bobby's shakes turned into tremors of terror.

It was bad enough to reach half-time without a goal. But that was only the beginning. In the second half, things got worse: much worse.

Chapter 8

A horribly familiar figure wheeled from the shadows: Kevin Joggs! I tensed up remembering how Kevin had mocked Bobby and I'd beaten his fat face into the mud. He'd deserved it. But I'd let Dad down. Now here he was again, just when I needed all my concentration.

He circled the park silently like a shark. I kept glimpsing his bike out of the corner of my eye, and that made me miss another good pass. I spied Kevin riding in towards Bobby. Then, at the last moment, he swerved. He'd spotted new prey.

I was relieved as he pedalled away, and I did a neat nutmeg round their defender. At last, I was finding my form. But just when I thought things were getting better, disaster struck – a dog barked. 'Charlie!' Bobby yelled in terror.

What should I do? I couldn't leave my team – not in the middle of a game, not with the goal in sight. But Bobby was my team.

The dog barked louder. It was getting nearer. And I was getting nearer to goal. Bobby shouted again, desperately.

Should I go to him? I had to chase the ball. Then, in the distance, I spotted Mr Maskell's wheelchair. He was sitting, helpless, and a bike was bearing down on him. Kevin was rearing up on his back wheel, whooping. The dog barked frantically. Bobby needed me.

'Help Mr Mascot!' he yelled.

'Charlie!' Fizza's shout cut in.

The ball dropped at my feet. I tore forwards, dashed past the last defender and walloped it into the back of the net.

Everyone cheered, high-fived, hugged. Sometimes I do a back flip when I score. But today I felt dreadful. I'd let my brother down. I'd let Mr Maskell down. It was the worst goal ever.

Chapter 9

The final whistle went. We'd won the cup! My team cheered and patted me on the back. I looked around but Bobby was nowhere to be seen. An eerie silence settled on the park. I ran from the pitch, afraid that at any moment killer dogs or dirty Joggs would leap out at me.

'Bobby, where are you?' I yelled.

Then I spotted Mr Maskell. Kevin had blocked the old man.

He was picking things out of the shopping basket and juggling with them. 'Smashing day.' He threw an egg at the pavement. 'Ooops – omelette,' he laughed. Then, with a mean smile, he snarled, 'I'm feeling eggy today – d'you like yours scrambled?' and he pulled back his arm, ready to fire.

'Stop!' I shouted, but I was too far away. I tripped and fell.

Then, from the mud, an amazing sight met my eyes. Bobby was tearing fearlessly across the grass. And Davy Dog was running towards him. For a second, Bobby froze. Then he pointed, and like brilliant footballers, the two separated and moved on Kevin from opposite sides. I couldn't believe it when Bobby dived. He pulled Kevin's feet clean off the ground and Joggsy was well and truly splatted. Davy jumped onto the fallen figure and barked triumphantly. By the time I reached them, Kevin was whimpering, 'Help, help – get him off me.'

Bobby was shaking a finger at him, saying, 'Naughty boy.'

'Well done, Bobby!' Mr Maskell beamed. 'I told you Davy was your special friend and he'd come to you for help.'

Bobby stared at the dog – suddenly shocked by his own bravery. He moved away from Davy and hid behind Mr M's chair.

Davy lay and waited.

'You see, he's puppy trained now,' Mr Maskell said to Bobby. 'He'll do what you tell him.'

'Stand,' Bobby tried, still keeping his distance. Davy got up and waited beside Kevin, who lay shaking in the mud.

'Sit,' Bobby said, trying out his new power. Davy sat.

Silently, Kevin started scrambling to his feet.

'Lie down,' Bobby ordered sternly. Kevin and Davy both dropped flat on their tummies. Bobby grinned.

'Now pick up the shopping and say sorry,' Bobby commanded.

Davy growled as Kevin gathered everything up, and mumbled, 'Sorry, sorry, sorry.' He cowered each time Davy barked. Bobby's eyes grew big as footballs as he saw Joggsy's fear.

'Now buy eggs,' Bobby said.

Snotty and tear-stained, Kevin raced from the park, with Davy yapping at his heels.

When Kevin had gone, Davy trotted up and sat obediently in front of Bobby and Mr Maskell.

Very nervously, Bobby reached out a hand and touched Davy. Then he pulled it away. Davy stayed still.

'Stand!' Bobby said.

Davy stood. A bit bolder, Bobby gave him a little stroke. Then a bigger one.

'Friends?' Bobby asked, and Davy wagged his tail.

'Now he's puppy trained, perhaps he's ready to start football training?' I suggested.

'Goalie?' Bobby asked.

'Yes, he's like you,' said Mr Maskell. 'A top defender!'

Bobby grinned from ear to ear.

'Run, Davy, run,' and the three of us ran out onto the pitch, Super Pup, Super Bobs and me.

About the Author

Sophie Smiley was born in a Dominican monastery – she says she had a very happy childhood surrounded by Fra Angelicos and Ethiopian priests! She now teaches English and is also a staff member of Forest School Camps, working with both the able and those with learning difficulties. She is married and has two children and they all live in Cambridge.

About the Illustrator

Michael Foreman is one of the most talented and popular creators of children's books today. He has won the Kate Greenaway Medal for illustration twice and his highly acclaimed books are published all over the world. He is married, has three sons and divides his time between St Ives in Cornwall and London.

Have you read the other books about Bobby, Charlton, and their football-mad family?

Bobby, Charlton and the Mountain

Bobby wants a football kit for the Queen's visit to his school! Money-making muddles, a beastly bully, and a breathtaking penalty shoot-out lead to a VERY unexpected meeting . . . !

ISBN 9781842701782 £4.99

Man of the Match

Bobby and Charlie are off to summer camp. As soon as Bobby sees Paul, he insists on being best friends with him, even though Paul hides under his parka. Of course Bobby insists on playing football with Paul whatever the planned activity really is. Charlie has her work cut out to keep track of them – and she has a big challenge of her own, too – a relay race over water, and she's petrified!

ISBN 9781842704202 £4.99

Team Trouble

Bobby and Charlie are terribly concerned when big-brother Semi gets ill. He becomes incredibly grumpy, and will only grunt at people – and worst of all, he doesn't seem to like football any more. Whatever can be wrong with him? Will the girl he meets mysteriously help bring him back into the family team?

ISBN 9781842706848 £4.99

Pirates Ahoy!

Charlie's football-mad family have moved their pitch to the beach, and her brother's on a quest for a pirate adventure. It's all hands on deck as footballs become cannonballs and damsels in distress are rescued. But will Bobby ever find his hidden treasure? And will Charlie even win him back to football?

ISBN 9781842708828 £4.99